P9-AGK-473

The Stone of Destiny

For my mother, Ann Rawstron,
who gave me a love of books and was always
an inspiration

Text copyright © Elspeth Tavaci 2012
Illustrations © Paul Hess 2012
The right of Elspeth Tavaci and Paul Hess to be identified as the author and
illustrator of this work has been asserted by them in accordance with the
Copyright, Designs and Patents Act, 1988 (United Kingdom).

First published in Great Britain in 2012 and in the USA in 2013 by
Frances Lincoln Children's Books, 4 Torriano Mews,
Torriano Avenue, London NW5 2RZ
www.franceslincoln.com

A catalogue record for this book is available from the British Library.

ISBN: 978-1-84780-279-8

Set in Minion and Weiss

Printed and bound by CPI Group (UK) Ltd, Croydon, CR0 4YY in April, 2012

1 3 5 7 9 8 6 4 2

The Stone of Destiny

Tales from Turkey

Elspeth Tavaci

Illustrated by
Paul Hess

F

FRANCES LINCOLN
CHILDREN'S BOOKS

Note on the name Istanbul

Over the centuries, this famous city has been called by 135 different names including Byzantion/Byzantium by the Ancient Greeks, Constantinople by the Romans, Konstantiniyye by the Islamic world, and Stambul in Arabic, Armenian and medieval writing.

Istanbul has been the city's common name throughout its history. The word comes from the Ancient Greek eis tin polin (meaning 'to the city'), which got shortened to stin poli. So Istanbul is the name I am using for these stories.

CONTENTS

❖ CHAPTER 1 ❖

Once there was and once there was not a poor stonecutter who lived on the faraway shores of the Black Sea, in a little town called Trabzon. You can still visit the town today. It nestles at the foot of the Kaçkar mountains, with a sparkling carpet of blue-black sea spread out before it.

In those long ago times, Trabzon was a small walled city on the great Silk Road which stretched from China in the east to Venice and Genoa in the west. Along that road came travelling caravans of camels carrying cargoes of treasures for padishahs and sultans, for princes and princesses, for kings and queens and for all the good people of Asia and Europe.

Our story begins one evening in June, when the sun sat like a huge orange ball suspended above the dark sea, spreading its pinky-orange glow over the little town of Trabzon. It was late, and soon the whole town would be blanketed by the soft bluey-blackness of a summer night. The chatter and clatter of dinnertime drifted from house to house through the now empty streets.

Everyone had gone home and the site where they were building a new mosque was deserted, but still the poor stonecutter worked.

"Just let me cut this one last boulder," Salahaddin thought, "and then I'll go home for dinner."

But Salahaddin the stonecutter never did go home for dinner. Suddenly the boulder split in two – and something caught his eye. A beautiful stone lay twinkling in its nest of rock, a deeper, darker red than the sun. Salahaddin lifted the stone out of the rock and held it up to the dying light. It was perfectly cut and not much smaller than an egg.

"How did something so beautiful come to be trapped inside this plain old boulder?" he wondered.

"Maybe a prince from an eastern land dropped it whilst travelling along the Silk Road." He mused for a moment. "Then, over the years, the stone embedded itself in the ground and now I, a stonecutter, have found it, and in time I will become richer than even the great sultan himself." And in his mind he quickly wove an enthralling story around the beautiful red stone.

For this was no ordinary stonecutter. No, this stonecutter was a storyteller who could weave a tale better than any carpet-weaver, who could find a story in the deepest, darkest depths of nowhere.

❖ CHAPTER 2 ❖

Salahaddin held the stone tightly in his hand and rubbed his finger over its smooth surface.

But wait a minute! The back was not smooth. There were tiny chips in the surface. He held it up again. There was some kind of inscription on the back of the stone but he couldn't read it.

"I'll take it to Ali. He'll know what it is," he thought, and he pushed the stone into the pocket of his robe. Then he ran up the narrow, winding cobbled street to the jeweller's shop.

By this time it was dark. He tried the door but it was locked. He peered in through the window and saw a flicker of light from an oil lamp at the back of the shop. Ali Usta was still there.

The stonecutter banged on the door. No sound. He banged again. Then he heard a shuffling and a muttering and he watched the old jeweller make his way to the front of the shop.

"Who is it?" the jeweller called.

"It's me, Salahaddin, the stonecutter."

"Ah, Salahaddin Usta." Salahaddin heard the bolt being drawn back. "What do you want at this time of night? Can't it wait till the morning?"

"Ali Usta," cried Salahaddin, "I have something wonderful to show you. I can't wait till the morning."

"Come in. Come in, my friend," said Ali Usta.

Old Ali shuffled to the back of the shop. Salahaddin followed, his hand turning the stone over in his pocket. Ali sat down at his small wooden workbench.

"Now, show me what all the fuss is about," he said. Salahaddin pulled the stone from his pocket and opened his hand.

The smile left Ali's face and the blood drained from his head to his toes as he stared at the beautiful rose-red stone. With a shaking hand, he took the stone from Salahaddin's outstretched palm.

"There is something inscribed on the back," said Salahaddin, "but I can't read it."

"Where did you find this?" asked Ali, his voice shaking as much as his hand. Salahaddin told him. Then Ali picked up his eye glass and put it to his eye. He picked up the stone and studied it for what seemed like forever.

"I am sorry," he said, with a sigh. "I can't read the script, but I believe I know what this stone is. It is the long-lost stone of King Comnenus, the last Byzantine king of Trabzon."

"The lost jewel!" said Salahaddin. "Yes, I know the story. I've told it many times. King Comnenus didn't want to pay taxes to Fatih Sultan Mehmet, the ruler of Istanbul, so he betrothed his beautiful daughter to a neighbouring ruler, Uzun Hasan Bey, on the understanding that the ruler would ask Fatih Sultan Mehmet to waive his taxes. Uzun Hasan Bey did as he asked. But he also told Fatih Sultan Mehmet that there was a debt owing to his ancestors and he wanted it repaid. Fatih Sultan Mehmet said that he would come

personally and pay back the debt – and he set off for Trabzon with his army.

"When Uzun Hasan Bey heard that the great sultan himself was coming, he was afraid, and sent his mother, Sara Hutun, to apologise to the sultan and ask his forgiveness. The sultan said he would forgive Uzun Hasan Bey – but nevertheless, he continued on to Trabzon; and, on hearing that the sultan was arriving with an army, King Comnenus surrendered the city. So Fatih Sultan Mehmet made Trabzon part of his empire, giving the jewels of the city to Sara Hutun to repay his debt."

"Told like a true storyteller," said Ali Usta.

"And you believe that this stone is one of those jewels?" said Salahaddin, hardly able to contain his excitement.

"Yes, I do. I do indeed," said Ali Usta.

"Then it is beyond price," said Salahaddin, and a big grin spread across his handsome face.

"Yes, beyond price. Now, listen carefully," said the old jeweller as he stared thoughtfully at the stone. "I have an old friend. He is a jeweller in the fine jewellery bazaar in Istanbul. He will be able to read the inscription and know what to do with the stone. You must leave for Istanbul immediately. Tell no one about the stone. Show no one. Trust no one. My friend's name is Osman Usta. When you get to the bazaar, ask for him. Now I bid you good night and good luck. And remember what I have said."

"Tell no one about the stone. Show no one. Trust no one," whispered Salahaddin, taking the stone back from the jeweller.

"Good, good. Ah, if only I was younger! I would come with you," said Ali Usta.

Salahaddin pushed the rose-red stone back into his pocket. He hugged the jeweller and bade him farewell. Then he ran up the cobbled street through the town and on to the bridge, where he stopped for a moment to catch his breath. And in that moment, he looked out across the town, his town – his home town, the place where he had lived and worked all nineteen years of his life. Then he took a deep breath and stretched out his arms as if he were about to fly, and his mouth stretched into a wide smile.

"My story begins here," he whispered into the wind.

Then he ran home, bubbles of excitement bursting from every pore in his body.

CHAPTER 3

When Salahaddin reached the house, his brother was sitting on the step outside.

"Saddle my horse," he called to his brother.

At the sound of Salahaddin's voice, his mother came out of the house.

"Where have you been? It's late. Come inside. Your dinner is on the table."

"Mother, I must leave immediately for Istanbul," Salahaddin said. "I have something for the Sultan."

"The Sultan . . . the Sultan?" his mother smiled. "Ah, I see – another of your stories. Save it until after dinner. Now, come inside, Salahaddin. You know I hate it when food goes cold."

"No, Mother, I can't. I really am going to Istanbul."

His mother looked into his determined green eyes and knew that nothing, not even her cheese and meat pastries, would stop him.

She sighed, and went inside to collect the clothes and food he would need for the journey. She filled his brightly woven saddlebag with more food than any man could ever hope to eat on one journey. Then she took it out to Salahaddin. He threw it over his white stallion's back and leapt into the saddle. He smiled down at her, dug his heels into the horse's flanks and was gone.

His mother stood and listened to the clip-clop of hooves on cobbles until silence swallowed them. Then she walked back into the house.

Salahaddin had never travelled much further than the city walls of Trabzon. But in his mind he had travelled far and wide. He had visited Mogul palaces in India, met padishahs in Persia and emperors in China. He had climbed snow-capped mountains and slain dragons and monsters. He had solved baffling mysteries and won the hearts of petulant princesses. He had swum across seas and sailed across oceans.

His father's voice was the vessel he travelled in, for Salahaddin's father had been a celebrated storyteller and had woven a magical world for his son to inhabit. All through his childhood, Salahaddin had sat and listened to his father's storytelling and in the flames of winter fires he had seen the great ships, the magnificent palaces, the beautiful princesses, the unconquerable kings and the mighty fortresses of these enchanting tales. Salahaddin had grown up believing that there was a wonderful world beyond the city walls just waiting for him, and now he was finally going to discover that world.

He rode through the dark velvety night, seeing no one and hearing no one, with only the stars for company. That is, no one except a young boy. A young boy with shoulders hunched, head bent and dusty worn-out sandals walking slowly along the side of the road.

"What is your name and where are you going, all by yourself?" called Salahaddin to the boy as his horse drew up beside him.

"My name is Hüseyin. I am going to Istanbul," replied the boy in a small voice.

"Give me your hand," said Salahaddin, and he stretched out his hand and pulled the boy up into the saddle behind him. "I, too, am going to Istanbul. We shall travel together."

And so they rode on, the tall, dark stonecutter and the thin, red-haired boy with pale freckled skin and blue eyes. No questions asked; the two travelled in silence, one with a heart full of sadness and the other with the thrill of adventure pounding through his veins. The white stallion thundered through the night like a falling star crossing the dark sky.

So determined were they to reach their destination that they hardly noticed what they ate or drank or where they slept. Daylight danced before their eyes to the rhythm of the horse's hooves and melted softly into the night.

On the twelfth night they stopped at the Durağan Caravanserai near Sinop.

A caravan of camels had arrived just before them, piled high with mysteries from the East. Caravans such as these criss-crossed the country with huge sacks of spices and bags of precious stones from India, pearls from Bahrain, incense and musk from Arabia, silk and porcelain from China, soaps from Syria and indigo, linen, rice and sugar from Egypt – on to Istanbul in the north-west, or south to the port of Antalya and from there across the seas to Genoa and Venice.

Salahaddin and Hüseyin dismounted and walked the last few metres to the caravanserai. Hüseyin gazed in wonder at the magnificent stone fortress before them. Salahaddin strode past the camels and up to the carved entrance gate with its strong iron door, bolted to keep out thieves or enemy armies. He banged on it. The bolt was drawn back, the door swung open, and a cacophony of sounds and smells burst out into the silent night. The guards stood to attention.

"Take their camels! You there, take this horse!" bellowed the porter. A groom hurried towards Hüseyin and led Salahaddin's horse off to be fed and watered. Salahaddin spoke to the innkeeper in the gatehouse and he and Hüseyin were given a place to sleep.

Hüseyin stared in wonderment at the scene spread out before him. "Come on," said Salahaddin. "You need a bath and a good hot dinner." He took Hüseyin's hand and led him through the hustle and bustle of the large open courtyard to the bath house. Words whirled around them in a confusion of languages ranging from Persian to Armenian, Venetian to Egyptian, Syrian to Maltese. The lyrical sounds melted into one magical language and Hüseyin longed to understand it.

❖ CHAPTER 4 ❖

The sounds followed them into the steamy bath house with its silvery-grey marble wash basins. They poured hot water over themselves with bath dippers and then lay on the huge hot marble slab waiting to be scrubbed and massaged by the masseur. Soft clouds of steam rose up into the huge dome above and shafts of light beamed down through its small star-shaped holes.

After the dust and dirt of their journey had been well and truly washed away, they went to have dinner. The caravanserai guests were sitting down to eat around a huge open fire in the courtyard. Salahaddin and Hüseyin joined them and ate a hearty meal of succulent lamb roasted in clay pots with freshly baked bread. The two ate in silence and watched the hubble-bubble of activity around them.

Still, Salahaddin didn't know why Hüseyin was going to Istanbul. "I'll ask him now," he thought, but when he looked down at Hüseyin and saw the sadness in his eyes, he decided not to. "This boy doesn't need reminding of his troubles," he thought, and he ruffled Hüseyin's hair. "What you need is a good story, Hüseyin. What do you think?"

"A story?" said Hüseyin, and his eyes lit up with excitement. "Yes, please!"

"A story . . . a story . . . he's going to tell a story." A wave of whispers whirled around the courtyard and one by one, group by group, the travellers were drawn towards Salahaddin until a huge circle of expectant faces bobbed before him. And just for a moment, Salahaddin thought he caught a glimpse of his father's dead face among them smiling up at him, waiting for the story to begin. . .

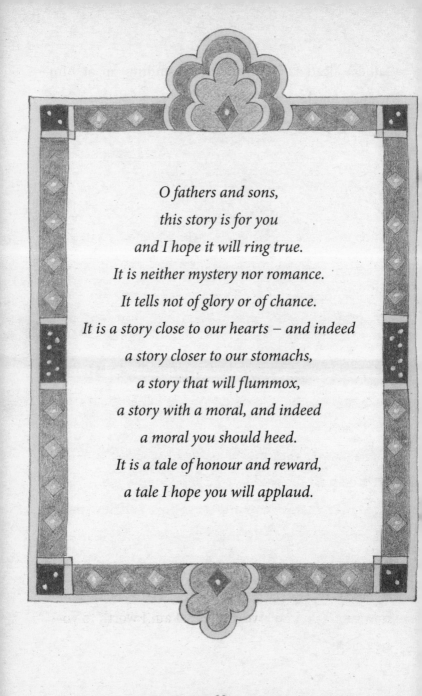

O fathers and sons,
this story is for you
and I hope it will ring true.
It is neither mystery nor romance.
It tells not of glory or of chance.
It is a story close to our hearts – and indeed
a story closer to our stomachs,
a story that will flummox,
a story with a moral, and indeed
a moral you should heed.
It is a tale of honour and reward,
a tale I hope you will applaud.

The Salt

Once there was, and once there was not a king. He was a fair king and he ruled his kingdom with justice, but unfortunately he was also a vain king who loved compliments. This king had three sons who were strong, intelligent and brave.

One day, the king called his eldest son. 'My dear son, how much do you love me? What am I worth to you?' he asked.

'I love you very much,' replied the eldest son. 'You are worth all the gold in your kingdom to me.'

The king was happy to hear this and he smiled. 'Thank you, my son,' he said. 'You obviously do love me very much.'

Then the king called his second son. 'My dear son, how much do you love me? What am I worth to you?' he asked.

'I love you very much,' replied the second son. 'You are worth all the silver in your kingdom.'

The king was happy and he smiled. 'Thank you, my son,' he said. 'You obviously do love me very much.'

Then the king called his youngest son, Timur. 'My dear son, how much do you love me? What am I worth to you?' he asked.

'I love you very much,' replied the youngest son. 'You are worth all the salt in your kingdom.'

When he heard this, the king was not happy. He frowned at his youngest son. 'Salt?' he roared. 'How *dare* you compare me to salt. Is that all I am worth in your eyes?'

'Yes, Father,' replied the young man. 'You are worth all the salt in your kingdom.'

'You ungrateful boy,' roared the king. 'Leave this palace at once.'

And so poor Timur left his father's palace. He took his camel and rode for days in the desert under the scorching sun until, one morning, something glinting in the sand caught his eye. He dismounted, and began to brush the sand away with his hands. There, just below the surface of the sand, lay a hoard of gold coins!

Timur couldn't believe his luck. He collected the coins together and stashed them in his saddlebag. He was now a very wealthy man and with the gold, he built himself a magnificent stone palace in the desert.

Many years passed, and both Timur and the king his father continued to live in their palaces. Then one day, the king went hunting in the desert and he caught sight of Timur's beautiful palace.

'Who owns this palace?' he asked his servants.

Nobody knew.

'Well, go and find out,' he roared.

And so the king sent his servants to the palace and they were welcomed there. Timur sent an invitation out to the king to join him. The king accepted, and rode over to the palace with his attendants. At once Timur recognised his father, but the king did not recognise his youngest son.

Timur ordered his chef to prepare an enormous feast, and told him not to put a single grain of salt in the food. The chef was surprised. 'Not a single grain? Are you sure?' he asked.

'Yes, I'm sure,' replied Timur. 'No salt!'

'Maybe just a little in the rice?' said the chef.

'No salt in anything,' said Timur. 'Not a single grain of salt in anything.'

'Very well,' said the chef, 'but the king will never want to dine here again and I will never get another job. I will be the laughing-stock of the kingdom,' he added grumpily.

That evening, the guests arrived and sat down at the table. The feast was served and all the hundreds of dishes looked wonderful. The guests' mouths watered when they saw the array of food.

The king took his first mouthful, and put his fork down on the table.

'There's no salt in this food. I can't eat food without salt. I'd give a silver coin for just a few grains of salt,' he said. Quickly a servant removed his dish from the table and took it back to the kitchen. Moments later, he returned the dish to the king with a smile. The king took a mouthful, and once again put his fork

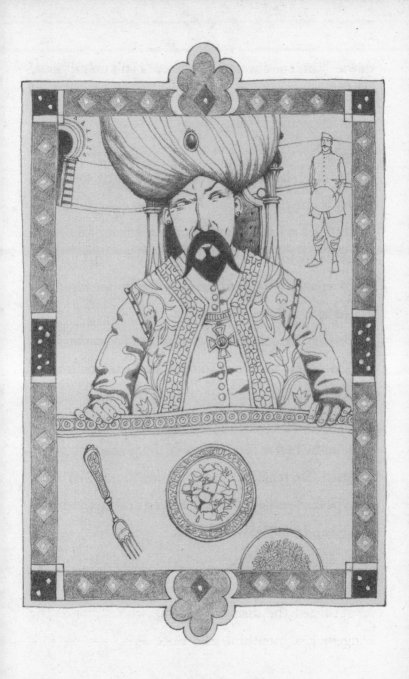

down. 'This food is inedible. There's still no salt in it,' he wailed. 'I'd give all the silver in my kingdom for just a few grains of salt' – for by this stage he really was hungry.

Quickly, the servant took the offending dish back to the kitchen. Moments later, he returned with it. The king took a mouthful and slammed his fork down on the table. 'Is there no salt in this palace? I can't eat this. I'll give you all the gold in my kingdom for just a few grains of salt,' he roared.

'So, Father,' said Timur, 'now at last you understand the value of salt. At last you see that it is worth more than gold and silver.'

At that, the king recognised his son, and he hugged him, for he had missed him over the years.

Then Timur called the chef. 'Bring the salt,' he cried, and the chef smiled, the king smiled and all the guests smiled and clapped their hands.

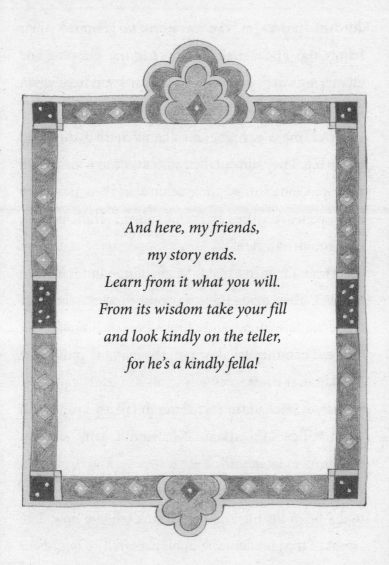

And here, my friends,
my story ends.
Learn from it what you will.
From its wisdom take your fill
and look kindly on the teller,
for he's a kindly fella!

All the guests at the caravanserai clapped their hands, too, and a huge wave of cheering, clapping and chattering swept across the courtyard and back again and slowly subsided into conversation.

After the story, the merchants settled down to bartering. They laid out their silks and linens, displayed their precious stones, their soaps and their porcelain and opened up their sacks of saffron, chilli pepper, cardamom and rice.

"Time for bed," said Salahaddin, and Hüseyin nodded. They made their way over to where the huge white stallion stood and climbed on to the platform above. Then they lay down on the mat and pulled the blanket over them.

Just as Salahaddin was about to fall asleep, a small voice beside him asked, "Salahaddin, why are you travelling to Istanbul?"

Now, Salahaddin was a truthful man. He had never told a lie in his life and he couldn't tell one now. The words of the jeweller rang in his ears: *Tell no one about the stone. Show no one. Trust no one.* But what was the harm in telling this boy? He was hardly likely to run off with the stone and, even if he did, he couldn't go far with it.

And so, against the jeweller's advice, Salahaddin told the boy the story of the stone.

The deep, rich tones of the stonecutter's voice carried the tale across to two Egyptian merchants who had just finished unsaddling their horses nearby. Perhaps there was no harm in this either, because merchants, after all, are respectable, honest citizens, are they not? The two men listened intently to the tale. "That stone must be worth a fortune," muttered one to the other, and they rubbed their hands together and twiddled their beards as they thought of the riches concealed in the storyteller's clothes.

Salahaddin and Hüseyin, blissfully unaware that anything was amiss, soon fell asleep to the neighing and baying of horses and donkeys and camels, the excited chatter and clatter, the laughter and strumming and drumming. But the two merchants lay awake plotting and scheming and dreaming of untold wealth, until dawn broke.

❖ CHAPTER 5 ❖

The two travellers woke up early to the smell of freshly baked bread. They washed quickly and then followed their noses. That morning they sat and shared a large crusty loaf of bread, a slab of creamy goat's cheese, salty black olives and sweet, syrupy honey. Neither paid much attention to the two merchants in wool cloaks with dark beady eyes, wiry grey beards and heavily bejewelled fingers who sat down beside them.

"Eh . . . hm," said one of the merchants. "Aren't you the storyteller?"

"Yes, yes, I am," said Salahaddin, looking up from his breakfast and smiling at the two men.

"Then it's a wonderful gift you have," continued the merchant.

"Thank you," said Salahaddin.

"One story is worth more than a cargo of precious stones, don't you think?" said the merchant, glancing down at the large emerald ring on his middle finger.

"Yes, that's so true," said Salahaddin, pleased to have found someone who, like himself, knew the value of a good story. Unfortunately, Salahaddin did not notice the greedy twinkle in the merchant's eyes but Hüseyin did, and he felt a shiver run through him. Salahaddin chatted on about his life in Trabzon, and Hüseyin silently watched the two men.

"So which way are you heading?" asked the first merchant.

"Northwest to Istanbul," Salahaddin replied.

"What a stroke of luck," said the merchant. "So are we. We have some business in the bazaar in Istanbul. Would you mind very much if we travelled with you? As you know, the road is a dangerous place. There are bandits, thieves and murderers roaming the country and we are on our own. We would feel much safer with you."

"Of course," said Salahaddin. He knew he would

not be able to travel as fast with two elderly men in tow but he couldn't refuse their request and, after all, what did it matter if he arrived in Istanbul a few days later than planned?

When the two merchants left to saddle their horses, Hüseyin begged Salahaddin not to let the two travel with them. "Whyever not?" asked Salahaddin.

"I have a bad feeling about them," said Hüseyin. "They're up to no good."

"Don't be silly, Hüseyin," said Salahaddin with a laugh. "They are good, honest men. I admit, they look a bit scary, but I'm sure they wouldn't harm a fly. Besides, nothing can happen to you whilst you're with me."

Hüseyin looked into Salahaddin's kind green eyes and he felt reassured. Salahaddin was right. Nothing could happen whilst he was with him. And so the four unlikely friends set off together. Up steep mountain roads and across grassy green plains they rode, the wind in their hair and adventure in their hearts.

After many days and nights of travelling, they came to the pretty little town of Safranbolu and walked

their horses through the narrow cobbled streets to the caravanserai known as Cinci Han. It was late and the streets were deserted. The only sound to disturb the sleeping townsfolk was the clip-clop of their horses' hooves on the cobbles.

Salahaddin rapped on the huge iron door of Cinci Han and they heard the scraping sound of the bolt being drawn back. When the door opened, the sounds within burst out like a cannon exploding into the night. The travellers were ushered in and given places for the night. It was cold, so they were offered a room in one of the galleries built around the courtyard.

❖ CHAPTER 6 ❖

All four travellers went to the bath house and washed away the dust and dirt and weariness of travel, then they tucked into a hearty meal. No sooner had the plates been cleared away, than Hüseyin's thoughts turned to stories.

"Salahaddin," said Hüseyin, "Can you tell us a tale?"

"Oh good gracious, no. It's been a tiring journey and we have another long journey ahead of us. I think we should all have an early night," said the tall, thin merchant, whose name was Talat.

"I agree," said Rifat, the shorter, plumper merchant. They had no wish to sit and listen to a bedtime story.

No, these two had more sinister things on their minds. They were both eager to return to their room, because the sooner Salahaddin and Hüseyin fell asleep, the sooner they could steal the stone and leave.

They needed a few hours' start. They were planning to head south-west to Afyon and on to Konya – which was their true destination. Konya was the city where the great Afghan poet Mevlana Jalaluddin Rumi had settled and made his home. It was the city where he had whirled and whirled whilst spinning words of wisdom into verse.

But, as before, the word 'story' flew from corner to corner, from bath house to tailor to blacksmith to money-changer and back again. Everybody wanted to hear a story. A musician strummed a tune on his strings. A drummer joined in, then a tambourine-player and a flute-player. People began to clap and chatter and the excitement in Cinci Han grew and grew, until finally the storyteller stood up and bowed. His audience clapped again, eager to encourage him.

Talat and Rıfat glared at the happy faces around them and mumbled and muttered at each other.

Nobody took any notice of the miserable men – nobody, that is, except Hüseyin. Their sullen faces and cold beady eyes sent a shiver of fear through him. He knew they were plotting something and he knew that it was something unpleasant.

Then Salahaddin began his story and all thoughts of danger slipped from Hüseyin's mind as the storyteller's magical words carried him away into a faraway world of princes and padishahs, princesses and palaces. . .

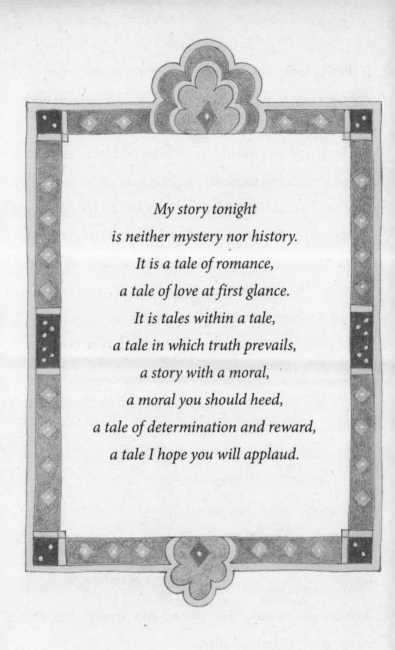

My story tonight
is neither mystery nor history.
It is a tale of romance,
a tale of love at first glance.
It is tales within a tale,
a tale in which truth prevails,
a story with a moral,
a moral you should heed,
a tale of determination and reward,
a tale I hope you will applaud.

The Prince, the Nightingale and the Silent Princess

Once there was and once there wasn't in a faraway land a padishah who had only one son.

His son grew bored sitting in the palace all alone with no one to talk to. 'I know, I'll buy a bird,' he thought. 'A bird will keep me company.'

So the prince went to the bazaar and bought a nightingale in a beautiful gilt cage. Pleased with himself, he took his new friend home and put the beautiful cage on the window ledge. Then he sat and waited for the  nightingale to sing. He waited and waited, but the nightingale remained silent.

One day, a swallow came and perched on the windowsill. When the nightingale saw the swallow, it said, 'Swallow, O swallow, pray weep for me, for I have lost my mate.'

When the prince heard the nightingale, he was surprised, because nightingales don't usually talk. 'So that's why you haven't sung for me – you're too sad to sing,' he said.

'Yes,' said the nightingale. 'A few months ago I lost my mate, and since then I have been too sad to sing.'

'At least you had a mate,' said the prince. 'The girl I wish to marry refuses to speak to anyone. Her father has said that unless I can get her to speak, I cannot marry her. Do you think you could help me make her talk? If you can, Allah might heal your grief.'

'Yes, perhaps I can help you,' said the nightingale. 'Tell me about this girl.'

'She is the most beautiful woman in the world,' said the prince. 'But that's not all. She's the cleverest woman in the world, too. She will not speak until she finds a man who is cleverer than she is. Whoever wants to marry her must persuade her to speak three times. Princes from all over the world have come to try and make her speak but her lips are sealed and not one word escapes them.'

For a minute the nightingale considered what the prince had told him. Then he said, 'Yes, I would be delighted to help you. We will go and see her tomorrow.'

The next morning, the prince got up early and dressed carefully. He tucked the nightingale into his jacket and set off for the silent princess's palace.

From her window, the princess watched him arrive.

'Huh!' she said to her maids. 'Here comes another fool to try and make me speak. Call him in, and let's see what he has to say for himself.'

When the prince entered the princess's chambers, he looked around and saw a small table with a lamp on it. Quickly he took off his red silk-embroidered slippers and placed them under the table. Then secretly, he slipped the nightingale into one of the slippers. The princess was sitting behind a heavy purple velvet curtain, so the prince couldn't see her.

'Good morning, table,' said the prince.

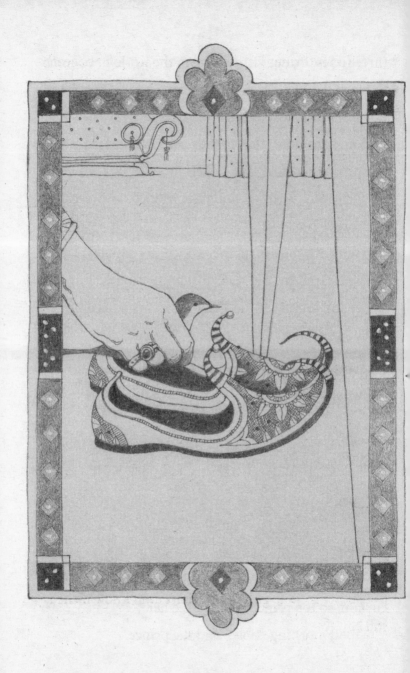

'Good morning,' said the nightingale from beneath the table.

They sat in silence for a moment or two.

'I do hate sitting in silence,' said the prince. 'It's so boring. Let's talk.'

'Very well,' said the nightingale. 'I will tell you a story.

'Once there were and once there weren't three friends who all wanted to marry the same girl. The girl said to them, "Go out into the world and work. Work hard and learn a special skill. Then come back at the end of the year. I will marry the man who has learnt the most unusual skill."

'The three men travelled far and wide. Each was determined to learn a special skill. At the end of the year, they returned to their country and met at a caravanserai near their journey's end.

'One of them said, "Listen, my friends. We all want to marry the same girl, but we don't even know if she is still alive."

'The second one said, "I have learnt the skill of hearing from a great distance. Let me listen, and find out how she is." Then he put his ear to the ground and listened very carefully. "Oh, no. I'm afraid I've got some very bad news," he said. "She is extremely ill. A doctor is with her now and he is trying to find a cure."

'"Don't worry," the third man said. "I have learnt the art of travelling great distances just by wishing myself there. Both of you, hold my hands tightly and I will take you to her."

'They did as he said. Then he closed his eyes and opened them again three times. Suddenly, the three friends found themselves outside the girl's house.

'"Come inside with me," said the first man. "I have learnt the art of healing every illness in the world." So the three men went inside. The first man laid his hand on the girl's forehead and instantly she was well again.'

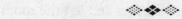

'Now,' said the nightingale, 'which of the three do you think the girl should marry?'

'In my opinion,' said the prince, 'she should marry the first man, because he cured her.'

'I disagree,' said the nightingale. 'I think she should marry the third man, because he was able to go immediately and help her.'

Behind the heavy velvet curtain, the princess clapped her hands together in excitement. 'No,' she said. 'You are both wrong. She should marry the second man, because he discovered she was ill and needed their help. If he hadn't done that, neither of the other two could have done anything to help her.'

The prince smiled. The princess had spoken. Now he felt sure he could make her talk again. Quickly he stood up. 'Well, table. I must be leaving now. It's been most interesting talking to you. I shall come again tomorrow.' Then he took the nightingale and slipped him into the pocket of his red silk kaftan. He put on his red silk-embroidered slippers and left the room.

As soon as he had gone, the beautiful princess came out from behind the curtain. 'Oh, girls,' she said to her maids, 'that clever young man has made me speak. He can even make a table talk.' She walked over to the table and said, 'Good morning, table.' But of course, the table didn't reply. 'Please say something,' said the girl, but the table remained silent.

The princess was angry with the table. 'Why do you talk to him and not to me?' she cried. 'Take the table away,' she said to her maids, 'then it can't talk to the prince again.'

'Now, girls,' she said, when the table had gone, 'I must not speak when that young man comes tomorrow. You must stop me. Put your hands over my mouth, if you have to. But please don't let me speak.' Her maids promised.

That night, the prince was overjoyed. The nightingale sang and he danced round the room. 'She spoke to us, little nightingale! She actually spoke to us! Allah willing, she'll speak to us again tomorrow.'

The next morning the prince got up even earlier and dressed with even greater care. He tucked the nightingale into the pocket of his silver-embroidered kaftan. Then he went to the palace and the servants showed him to the princess's chamber.

The prince looked about the room. 'Oh!' he said. 'The table has gone. Never mind. I shall talk to this chair instead.' And he took off his silver silk-embroidered slippers and put them under the chair. Then he placed the nightingale inside one of the slippers.

'Good morning, chair!' he said, as he sat down on a huge cushion.

'Good morning to *you*, my prince!' answered the nightingale from beneath the chair.

They sat in silence for a moment or two. Then the prince said, 'I really do hate sitting in silence. It's so boring. Let's talk.'

'Very well," said the nightingale. "I will tell you a story.

'Once there were and once there weren't in a faraway land three friends who were travelling to Baghdad together. It was a long and arduous journey. On and on they rode, until one evening they found themselves at the edge of a deep, dark forest. Afraid to go any further, they decided to spend the night there. "You both go to sleep, and I'll keep watch for the first hour," said the first friend. "Then I'll sleep while one of you stands guard. We'll take it in turns to keep watch until dawn."

'The first friend was a wood-carver. To keep himself amused while he stood guard, he cut a piece of wood from one of the trees and began carving a doll out of the wood. And in just one hour, he had finished making a beautiful doll! He stood it up against a tree and woke the second guard. Then he fell asleep.

'Now, the second man was a tailor. When he woke up and saw the doll, he said, "Ah, what a beautiful doll. I'll make a dress for her." He placed all their hats and his cloak in a pile and collected some thorns from the bushes nearby. When that was done, he sat down and pulled out his scissors. Skilfully he began to cut the hats and the cloak into small pieces. Then he put the pieces together and neatly attached them with thorns to make a dress for the doll. By the end of the hour, the doll was wearing a delightful dress! He stood the doll up against a tree. Then he woke

the third friend, and he fell asleep.

'The third friend was a priest. When he saw the beautifully-dressed doll, he said, "Ah, what a pity this doll is not alive." He decided to pray to Allah to bring the doll to life. He prayed a long and heartfelt prayer, and, lo and behold, before he had finished his prayer, the doll was alive and breathing!'

'Now,' the nightingale asked the prince, 'which man do you think deserves to marry the girl?'

The prince answered, 'The priest, of course, because he brought her to life.'

'No, I disagree,' said the nightingale. 'I think she should marry the tailor, because he dressed her so cleverly.'

The silent princess heard all this from behind the heavy velvet curtain.

'No, no. You are *both* wrong,' she said. 'She should marry the wood-carver, because he was the one who created her.'

All her maids ran towards her and put their hands over her mouth, but she pushed them away, saying, 'No! I disagree, and I must say what I think is true.'

Of course, the prince was ecstatic to hear the princess speak a second time. He took the nightingale from his slipper and tucked it into the pocket of his silver silk-embroidered kaftan. Then, after he had put on his silver silk-embroidered slippers, he left the room.

The moment he had gone, the princess cried, 'Oh, *why* did you let me speak?'

And her maids replied, 'What could we do? We tried to stop you, but you were determined to speak.'

Now the princess was even angrier than before. She pushed the purple velvet curtain aside and stormed over to the chair. 'Good morning, chair!' she said in a loud, clear voice. There was silence. 'Good morning!' she said again.

But of course the chair didn't answer because, as we all know, chairs can't speak, can they?

'Oh, why won't you talk to me?' said the girl. The maids all held their breath but there was silence.

She went on, 'I suppose you, too, only talk to clever princes.'

Of course, the chair didn't answer, so the princess asked one of her maids to take the chair away. 'I never want to see it again,' she said.

As for the prince, he had gone home a very happy man. He was confident that he could persuade the silent princess to talk a third time.

The next day, the prince got up early and dressed with the greatest of care. He tucked the nightingale into the pocket of his golden, silk-embroidered kaftan. Then he went to the house of the beautiful girl. The servants opened the door and showed him to the princess's chambers.

When he looked around the room, he saw that the chair had gone. He found a small bench in one corner and put his golden silk-embroidered slippers under it. Gently, he tucked the nightingale into one of the slippers. Then he sat down on a huge cushion.

'Good morning, bench!' he said cheerfully.

And, 'Good morning to *you* too, my prince!' answered the nightingale from beneath the bench.

They sat in silence for a moment or two. Then the prince said, 'I hate sitting in silence. Let's talk.'

'Very well,' answered the nightingale. 'I'll tell you a story.

'Once there was and once there wasn't in a distant land the daughter of a wealthy landowner. The family had a freed slave, and as children, the slave and the landowner's daughter had become very good friends. One day, when they were both eighteen, the slave asked the girl's parents if he could marry her. But the landowner refused to let the slave marry his daughter.

'The following day, the freed slave said to the girl, "I asked your father if I could marry you, but he said no. I must leave your family now and work for myself."

'The girl was upset when he left and sorely missed her friend. The freed slave went to work as a shepherd. He worked hard and soon he was able to buy some sheep for himself.

'Then he worked even harder, and soon he was able to buy a piece of land. Then he worked harder still, and soon he was the wealthiest landowner in the kingdom. Then he went back to the landowner and asked again for his daughter's hand in marriage.

' "You are the third man to come and ask for her hand in marriage," said the landowner. "My wealthy neighbour's son and, indeed, the padishah's son have both asked to marry her." '

'Now, tell me,' said the nightingale, 'who do you think the landowner's daughter should marry?'

'The wealthy neighbour's son, of course,' said the prince, 'because he is from the same background as the landowner's daughter.'

'I disagree,' said the nightingale. 'I think she should marry the padishah's son.'

When the silent princess heard this from behind the curtain, she clapped her hands and cried, 'No, no! You are wrong. She should marry the freed slave because he has worked hard and shown that he truly loves her.'

While she was talking, her maids tried to stop her

but they couldn't. 'Truth is not dead in the world,' she said. 'It is meant to be spoken.'

Then the prince said quietly, 'The silent princess has spoken three times. She must now become my bride.'

The velvet curtain was drawn aside and the princess stood there before him, as beautiful as the fourteenth day of the moon. She sat down on a cushion beside him and they talked together.

'I am the son of a padishah,' said the prince, 'and I have everything that we need to enjoy a comfortable life. Bring with you only those things which you want most, things light in weight but heavy in value. I shall go ahead and give the good news to my parents.'

Then he went to the bench and, reaching beneath it, took out his golden silk-embroidered slippers. Gently slipping the nightingale into the pocket of his gold silk-embroidered kaftan, he put on his slippers and left the room.

Once the prince was outside, he reached into his pocket for the nightingale. 'Go, my little friend,' he said. 'Fly free. Find a new mate. Bring joy to others as you have brought joy to me. Go! And may Allah go with you.' And he watched as the nightingale flew away. Then he travelled home to tell his parents the happy news of his marriage.

In good time, the prince came back to fetch the princess, her maids and her most precious possessions and together they travelled to his father the padishah's palace. There they had a most magnificent wedding that lasted forty days and forty nights, and they lived happily ever after.

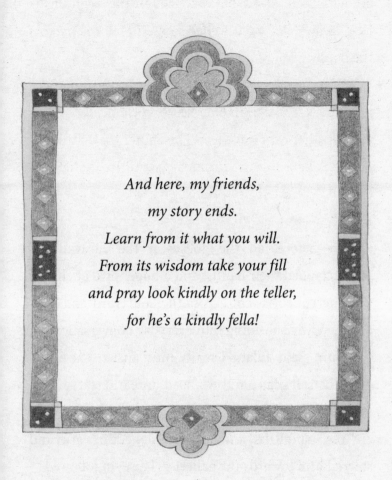

And here, my friends,
my story ends.
Learn from it what you will.
From its wisdom take your fill
and pray look kindly on the teller,
for he's a kindly fella!

❖ CHAPTER 7 ❖

As before, all the guests at the caravanserai clapped their hands, and a huge wave of chatter and merriment swept across the courtyard and back again, slowly subsiding into everyday conversation.

"Now," said Talat. "I really must insist that we all go to bed. It's late, and we need an early start in the morning."

"Yes," said Rıfat, and he took Salahaddin's arm and steered him towards the galleries. Hüseyin followed.

"You are right, my friends," said Salahaddin. "I, too, am eager to reach Istanbul."

And so the four travellers settled down to sleep. But Hüseyin couldn't sleep. Something was wrong.

Why didn't he feel comfortable with the two merchants? Salahaddin trusted them without question, so why didn't he? He lay still on his bed and listened to the snores from the other side of the room. "Maybe, if I retell Salahaddin's story to myself, I'll fall asleep," he thought. And so he began *Once there was and once there was not in a faraway land . . .* but he got no further than that – because one of the beds creaked at the other side of the room and a shadow moved silently along the pale stone wall towards Salahaddin's bed. Hüseyin gripped his blanket and peeped over the top. Rıfat was standing at Salahaddin's bedside. His bejewelled fingers were searching Salahaddin's saddlebag.

"What are you doing?" cried Hüseyin. The merchant froze, and Salahaddin sat bolt upright in bed. "Yes, what's going on?" asked Salahaddin sleepily.

"He's trying to steal the stone," said Hüseyin.

"Stone, what stone? What would Rıfat want with an old stone?" said Talat from his bed. Rıfat stood frozen near Salahaddin's saddlebag. "I'm afraid Rıfat sleepwalks," Talat went on. "He doesn't know what he's doing when he's sleepwalking. I'm sorry

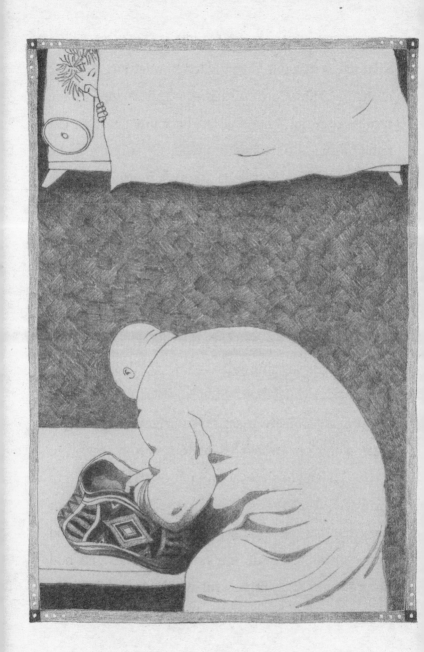

he has disturbed you both." The merchant got up, went to his friend and gently led him back to his bed, where Rıfat lay down and pretended to sleep. "It's a terrible affliction," said Talat. "I once found him sitting in a fountain. He had no idea where he was or why he was there. After that, the poor man had terrible flu. He had to stay in bed for a week."

"I see," said Salahaddin. "Yes, poor man. It is indeed a terrible affliction. Now, I suggest we all try and go back to sleep."

"But, Salahaddin. . ."

Salahaddin squeezed Hüseyin's hand, urging him not to say anything more.

"Go to sleep now, Hüseyin. We'll talk in the morning," said Salahaddin firmly. And so they all lay there with their private thoughts swirling around in the darkness. Salahaddin had not believed a word of the merchant's story, but he knew he could not accuse this respected pillar of society of lying. No one would believe him if he said, "This man is a thief." He had no proof – and what was his word against that of a respected merchant twice his age. Besides, he had not lost the stone. It was still there in the pouch hanging round his neck, hidden beneath his shirt.

As for the merchants, they were angry because they had not succeeded in stealing the stone, and it was all that pesky red-haired boy's fault.

Hüseyin was now determined to stay awake and keep guard over the stone. He was not going to let those two men steal it from his friend. He would rather die first.

And so they all lay there wide awake, waiting for dawn.

In the morning, Hüseyin and Salahaddin got up first and went to wash. As soon as they left the room, the two merchants began scheming.

"I've got another idea," said Rıfat. "We'll tell some of the other guests about the stone and ask them to stop us on the road and rob us."

"That's a stupid idea," said Talat. "If they rob us, they will end up with the stone and we won't. What's to stop them riding off with it? I don't think we should tell anyone else about it. Besides, I have a better idea. We could put a sleeping draught in their drinks tomorrow evening at supper. Then, when we look for the stone, that pesky boy won't wake up."

"But where are you going to get a sleeping draught?"

"I'll go and see the doctor. I'll tell him I'm having trouble sleeping. You leave it to me. By this time tomorrow we'll have the stone and we'll be on our way to Konya," replied Talat, with a smug grin on his face.

Meanwhile, Salahaddin and Hüseyin were discussing their travelling companions. "I'm sure they were trying to steal the stone," said Hüseyin. "Let's leave without them."

"But how did they know about it?" asked Salahaddin. "I haven't told anyone about it except you and Ali Usta."

"They probably overheard you telling me," said Hüseyin. "Your voice is distinctive. It must have carried to where they were sitting."

"Even if they do know about the stone, we can't know for sure that they intend to steal it," said Salahaddin, who was always ready to see the best in people. But the words of Ali Usta rang in his ear again – *Tell no one about the stone. Show no one. Trust no one* – and he instantly regretted telling Hüseyin the story.

"In future, I will have to be more careful," he said out loud. "If I had followed Ali Usta's advice in the first place, none of this would have happened. It is all my fault. Still," he mused, "a promise is a promise. If they still want to travel with us, then so be it. I can't leave them to travel by themselves. And now we know that they may be trying to steal the stone, we will be more vigilant."

"Very well," said Hüseyin. "If that's what you wish, then so be it. You have been so kind to me, and I won't be the one to stop you from showing kindness to others."

Salahaddin gave Hüseyin a hug and then, after they had finished washing, they made their way to breakfast.

The two merchants greeted them as if nothing had happened the previous night. In fact, nobody mentioned the incident. The four went about their preparations for the journey. As they were about to leave, Talat said to Salahaddin, "I'm just going to pop to the doctor's and get a sleeping draught for my friend here. Then, hopefully, he won't sleepwalk again and we can all sleep peacefully in our beds."

"Very well," said Salahaddin, "we'll be waiting for you outside." The merchant hurried off to see the doctor and Salahaddin saddled his white stallion and helped Hüseyin into the saddle. Then he led him out through the huge, ornate stone gateway into the street outside. Rifat followed with the other two horses.

Soon Talat came hurrying out clutching a small pouch. "I have the powder," he said happily. "We shall all sleep well tonight." Then the two men and Salahaddin mounted their horses and followed the colourful caravan of camels, horses, donkeys and mules down the windy narrow streets to the gates of the town.

That day and the next, the journey passed as journeys had before, and they rode on towards Bursa with the wind in their hair and adventure in their hearts.

❖ CHAPTER 8 ❖

The days sped by in a clatter of horses' hooves until one evening, saddle sore and weary, the four travellers reached the town of Bursa. As they rode into the town, the call to prayer echoed back and forth across the majestic city in an invisible chain of sound linking one mosque to another. And in the dusky light, the travellers made their way through the winding cobbled streets to Yeşil Cami, the Green Mosque, for evening prayers.

Salahaddin had never seen anything quite so stunning as this magnificent marble mosque with its huge arched windows, and pretty patterned tiles in the sunshine colours of sky and sea. He gazed at the vivid

emerald greens, tranquil turquoises, brilliant blues and whites of soft clouds on a sunny day.

The travellers performed their ablutions in silence, took off their shoes and stepped inside the magnificent mosque. Hüseyin stared up in awe at the vaulted ceilings and domed roof. The light from hundreds of lanterns twinkled like stars above his head, throwing shadows across the marble pillars and intricate geometric patterns on the walls.

After prayers, they stood for a while outside the great mosque and looked out across the higgledy-piggledy red-tiled roofs and tall tapering minarets of the city of Bursa, and beyond to the grassy plains.

"Who's hungry?" asked Salahaddin.

"I am," said Hüseyin.

Salahaddin enquired about accommodation and was told to head for Koza Han, the largest and grandest caravanserai in the city. For the past two and a half centuries Koza Han had been the centre of the silk trade. Every year in June and July, the farmers brought sacks of white silk cocoons to the city to sell. And every year the merchants came along the Silk Road from far and wide to buy the silk cocoons.

That evening, as they sat in the great courtyard, Talat brought them glasses of rich red pomegranate juice. He gave one to Salahaddin and one to Hüseyin. Then he gave one to Rıfat and took one himself.

Hüseyin took a large gulp of his pomegranate juice and Salahaddin raised his glass to his lips, but before he could take a sip, Hüseyin said, "Are you going to tell us a story, Salahaddin?" As before, the word "story" flew back and forth across the courtyard and in seconds, a crowd of expectant faces had gathered around Salahaddin.

He put down his glass, spilling some as he did so. A cat ran over and lapped up the spilt juice. Hüseyin ruffled its fur and gathered it into his lap, where the cat lay contentedly.

Talat grimaced when he saw Salahaddin put the glass down. "Patience," he thought. "There is still time for him to drink it."

Salahaddin had not even sipped the pomegranate juice, but the rich red liquid reminded him of a story he had not told for a long time. . .

My story tonight:
a tale of success
and a wedding dress,
a tale of true love
and all the above,
a tale of reward,
a tale I hope you'll applaud.

All for a Wrinkled Little Pomegranate

Once there was and once there was not a long time
ago a padishah of India who had a beautiful daughter
called Gülsün. And in Iran a padishah who had a
handsome son called Hasan.

The padishah of Iran sent an envoy to India. 'My
friend,' he said, 'let us marry my son to your daughter.'
The padishah of India agreed. And so the marriage
was arranged.

No one had ever been to such a magnificent
wedding. For forty days and forty nights there were
feasts and celebrations.

Then, on the morning of the forty-first day, Prince
Hasan and his bride and all her belongings left in a
long procession for Iran.

On the way, Prince Hasan spotted a wrinkled little
pomegranate lying by the side of the road.

'Stop, my princess,' he said. And while Gülsün watched, he got off his horse and bent down to pick up the pomegranate. He dusted it off, broke it open and offered half to her.

'I can't eat that!' said Gülsün disdainfully. She was most offended, because she was rather proud. 'I would never pick anything up from the roadside and eat it! And I can't live for the rest of my life with a prince who would do such a thing.'

Then she turned her horse's head and rode back to India.

Well, as you can imagine, Prince Hasan was surprised. And as for the padishah of Iran, he was annoyed. There on the spot he arranged an engagement between his son and another princess.

But Hasan could not forget the beautiful girl he had married. He was sure he didn't want to marry anybody else. 'But first,' he said to himself, 'I must teach her not to be so proud.'

He took off his fine clothes and put on an old shirt and some tattered trousers. Then, disguised as a gardener, he set off on the long journey for India.

On the way, he let his beard grow longer and scruffier to complete his disguise. When he arrived, he went straight to the palace of the padishah.

'Your Majesty,' he said, 'I am a hard-working gardener. Please let me work for you.'

The padishah liked Hasan's manner and agreed to hire him. His visir's servant showed Hasan to a small hut at the bottom of the garden. 'You can live here,' he said. 'There's a straw mat for you to sleep on, and you can eat your meals in the palace kitchen.'

The prince, who was fond of gardening, went to work immediately, and he did indeed prove himself to be a fine gardener. Soon the garden became a magical place.

Even the princess noticed the change in the garden and she began to spend more time there.

One day, Hasan was singing to himself as she walked there, and he made sure that she heard his song.

'If you love roses, a beauty you must be.
Smile, my princess, so my luck will smile on me.
Oh, don't be cross, fair princess, if I tell you
the name of my sweetheart is Gülsün too.'

'Oh!' she thought. 'So the gardener is in love with a girl called Gülsün. Surely it won't do any harm just to talk to him for a while.' And so the princess and Hasan chatted about the garden. After that, Gülsün went to the garden to talk to the gardener every day, and before long she had fallen in love with him. And of course, he was already in love with her.

'My princess,' he said to her one day, 'what shall we do? Your father will never allow us to get married.'

'Then let's run away together,' she said, 'because I don't want to marry anybody but you.'

So one night when no one was about, they eloped together on a horse that Gülsün took from her father's stable.

While they were riding along, Hasan saw a broken comb by the roadside. 'Oh, a comb!' he exclaimed. 'That's lucky! Get down and pick it up, my love.'

'But it's broken,' said Gülsün. 'I don't want a broken comb.'

'My dearest,' he said patiently, 'I have told you that I am poor. I can't afford to buy you a comb. Hurry and pick it up, then we can go.'

Gülsün really didn't want the comb. After all, she was a proud princess, but she loved Hasan and she wanted to make him happy. So reluctantly, she got down off the horse, picked up the broken comb and put it in her saddlebag. Then they went on their way.

A little farther along, Hasan saw a dented bath dipper. 'Oh, a bath dipper!' Hasan exclaimed. 'That's lucky! Quickly, get down and pick it up, my love.'

'That dented old bath dipper?' she asked. 'I don't want an old bath dipper.'

'My dearest,' he said gently, 'I have told you how poor I am. I can't afford to buy you a bath dipper. Hurry and pick it up, so that we can go.'

Gülsün really didn't want the bath dipper. After all, she was a proud princess, but she loved Hasan and she wanted to make him happy. So she got down off the horse, picked up the bath dipper and put it in her saddlebag. Then they went on their way again.

A little farther along, they came upon a torn old bath wrap. 'Oh, a bath wrap!' Hasan exclaimed. 'That's lucky! Quickly, get down and pick it up, my dearest.'

'But it is torn and full of holes,' Gülsün said.

'I don't want a tattered old bath wrap.'

'My dearest,' he said cheerfully, 'I have told you how poor I am. I can't afford to buy you a bath wrap to take to the bath house. Hurry and pick it up, so that we can go.'

This was almost too much for the princess's pride, but she loved Hasan and she wanted to make him happy. So she got down off the horse, picked up the torn old bath wrap and put it in her saddlebag. Then they went on their way again.

As soon as they could, they found a priest to marry them. Oh, how happy they were!

Then on they rode until they came to the palace of the padishah of Iran.

'Welcome to your new home,' said Hasan, getting down from his horse.

'But this is the padishah's palace,' replied the puzzled princess. 'We can't possibly stay here. Someone might recognise me.'

'No one will recognise you in these clothes, my sweet. Let me explain. Before I left India, I worked here at the palace as a gooseherd. And when I left, I promised the padishah that I would come back.

On the journey to India I needed to work, so I found odd jobs as a gardener and finally, as you know, I found a job at your father's palace. Now, follow me and I'll show you your new home.' And Hasan led her to a little goose coop with a patched roof and mud floor. Over in the corner were two straw mats to sleep on.

'I know it's not ideal,' he said, 'but we'll manage. You must be patient, my dearest.' And because the princess loved him, of course she was patient. They had bread and cheese and olives to eat, and tea to drink, and they were happy together.

Then one afternoon, Hasan came home and said to Gülsün, 'The padishah's son is going to get married, and the cooks in the kitchen need someone to help them sort the rice tomorrow for the wedding banquet. I said that you would go and help them, my dearest.'

'Of course,' she agreed.

'Just before you leave, slip a few handfuls of rice into your pockets to bring home,' he said.

'What! Do you want me to steal?'

'Don't worry,' he replied. 'The padishah has so much rice that a few handfuls will never be missed.

We can make soup with it.'

Well, the next day Gülsün went to the palace kitchen to sort rice. She sorted and sorted, and worked hard all day. Then, just before she was ready to leave, she slipped two handfuls of rice into each of her pockets.

Now earlier that day, Hasan had asked the cook to search the gooseherd's wife.

As Gülsün walked to the door, the chief cook came over and said, 'My girl, we must search your pockets. Sometimes girls steal the rice, you know.' And when he searched her pockets, there was the rice.

'For shame!' said the cook. 'If you had asked us for rice, we would have given you some. But stealing is a terrible thing!'

Gülsün left, feeling ashamed, and hurried home to her husband. 'How could you make me do such a thing?' she cried. 'They searched me and found the rice. I'm so humiliated!'

'Don't worry, my dearest,' Hasan said gently. 'Remember, I'm a poor gooseherd and we haven't much food. It's not such a terrible thing for us to take a little food now, is it?' And his words made her feel better.

A few days later, Hasan came home with the news that the next day, seamstresses at the palace were going to make the bride's dresses. 'I want you to go there and help them tomorrow, my dearest,' he said. 'And before you come home, hide a few metres of cloth under your shawl and bring it home with you. If we have a baby, we'll need some cloth to make baby clothes.'

'I shall go,' she said, 'but I won't steal any cloth. You know what happened with the rice.'

'Don't worry, my love,' he said. 'Just do as I say. They won't find you out this time.'

So the next day Gülsün went to help with the dresses. She worked hard all day long. Then, just before she was ready to leave, she hid a few metres of cloth under her shawl.

But again, Hasan had asked the palace women to search Gülsün before she left, and again they found that she had stolen something.

'Oh, my dear girl, how can you do such things?' they exclaimed. 'If you need cloth, all you have to do is ask. But stealing is a terrible thing!'

Gülsün hurried home to her husband. 'Oh, I'm

so ashamed!' she cried. 'They searched me again today, and they found the cloth I had hidden in my blouse. I will never steal again.'

'Don't get upset, my sweet,' he said calmly. 'You know I am only a poor gooseherd. We could never afford to buy clothes for our child, so it's not such a terrible thing to take a little piece of cloth. And, after all, they didn't punish you, did they? You see, they expect such things of a gooseherd's wife.'

His words made her feel a little better.

A few days later, Hasan came home with the news that the next day, the seamstresses were going to sew beads and coins onto the bride's dresses. 'I want you to go and help, my dearest. And this time, just before you leave, hide a gold coin under your tongue. No one will ever find it there.'

'No,' she said, 'I *won't* steal again.'

'Sweetheart, one gold coin is nothing to the padishah of Iran.'

'I can't do it,' she said.

'If you love me, you will,' he said.

And so the next morning, she went to the palace

to help the seamstresses sew beads and coins on to the bride's dresses. And just before she left, she hid a gold coin under her tongue.

Now, Hasan had asked his mother, the padishah's wife, to search the gooseherd's wife. So, just as Gülsün was leaving, the padishah's wife said, 'I'm afraid I must search you.' She searched Gülsün's pockets and, finding nothing there, ordered her to open her mouth. And of course she found the coin.

'Have you no pride at all?' exclaimed the padishah's wife. 'Stealing is a terrible crime.' And she sent Gülsün back to the goosecoop.

When she arrived home Gülsün was crying. 'How could you do this to me?' she said. 'The padishah's wife herself searched me and found the gold coin. I'm so ashamed. I can never go back to the palace again – never!' And she wept, and would not be comforted.

Two days later it was time for the wedding bath. 'Look, my dearest,' Hasan said, 'all the women are going to the bath house. There won't be any charge for bathing today. You should go and wash before the wedding too.'

'How can I go?' she asked. 'I don't have a comb or a bath dipper or even a bath wrap. How can I go to the bath house?'

'Whatever happened to the comb and the bath dipper and the bath wrap that we found?' Hasan asked.

Well, Gülsün cried and protested, but at last she agreed to go to the bath house. She arrived before everyone else and sat nervously in a dark corner where she hoped no one would notice her. She wrapped herself in the torn old bath wrap, rinsed herself with the dented old bath dipper and combed her hair with the broken old comb.

While she was washing, the bride-to-be and her party arrived. They feasted on peaches and pomegranates and all kinds of delicious pastries and they laughed and chatted and had a good time. The bride-to-be was wrapped in a gold-embroidered bath wrap. Her maids rinsed her with a golden bath dipper and combed her hair with a golden comb.

While the bride-to-be was being pampered and preened, the padishah's son, now dressed in clothes befitting a prince and with his beard and moustache

neatly trimmed, brought a tray to the door of the bath house. On the tray was a gold coin, some Turkish delight, a rose, a thorn and a wrinkled little pomegranate.

'This is a riddle,' he told the bathhouse-keeper. 'Whoever guesses the answer to this riddle will be my true bride.'

'You can't be serious!' exclaimed the bathhouse-keeper. 'Your bride-to-be is in the bath house now with her bridal party.'

'You heard what I said,' insisted the prince. 'Ask everyone in the bath house this riddle, beginning with the girl who calls herself my bride.'

So the bathhouse-keeper took the tray into the bath house. First she asked the bride-to-be and then every member of the bridal party the riddle, but no one could guess the answer.

She took the tray back to the prince. 'No one could answer it, Your Majesty,' she said.

'Try again,' insisted the prince. 'My wife must be able to guess this riddle – or she is not truly my wife.'

And so the bathhouse-keeper took the tray round the bath house again. First she asked the bride-to-be and then the rest of the bridal party, but still, no one could guess the answer to the riddle. Once again the bathhouse-keeper took the tray back to the prince.

'Are you sure you have asked everyone?' said the prince.

'Well, I didn't ask the gooseherd's wife,' admitted the bathhouse-keeper.

'Then ask her,' said the prince. 'After all, she is a person too, isn't she?'

So the bathhouse-keeper carried the tray to the darkest corner of the bath house. 'Here is a riddle,' she said. 'Can you answer it?'

Gülsün looked at the articles on the tray. Then she said,

'Ah, once as precious as gold was I,
and as sweet as lokum*, too;
from the only rose in a garden of joy
to a common thorn I grew,
and the only cause for this change in guise
in a wrinkled little pomegranate lies.'

* *Turkish Delight*

The bathhouse-keeper hurried back to the prince and said, 'The gooseherd's wife has an answer to your riddle,' she said. And she repeated the rhyme.

'Then,' said the prince, 'she is the girl I will marry.'

'But that's impossible!' exclaimed the bathhouse-keeper. 'Your bride-to-be is already being bathed for the wedding. Besides, the gooseherd's wife is already married.'

'You heard what I said,' the prince insisted. 'Get the gooseherd's wife bathed and dressed and bring her to me.'

So the bathhouse-keeper and the bride-to-be's attendants wrapped the gooseherd's wife in the gold-embroidered bath wrap and rinsed her with the golden bath dipper and combed her hair with the gold comb.

'What's going on? What are you doing?' Gülsün kept asking.

'The padishah's son is going to marry you,' they answered.

'But I am already married to the gooseherd, and I love him very much. I will not marry the prince!'

Still they kept washing her, and afterwards they

dressed her in one of the bride's new dresses. She wept the whole time. And of course the bride-to-be was weeping too, but for a completely different reason!

The prince called for a carriage to take Gülsün to the palace, where she was given a magnificent room.

In the evening, the prince visited her. When Gülsün saw Prince Hasan she recognised him, but was adamant that she didn't want to marry him. 'I am already married,' she wept. 'I don't want another husband.'

The prince left the room. He put on his tattered old gooseherd's clothes and then he came back. Gülsün stared at him in surprise and disbelief.

'You see, my dearest,' he said, 'I am both the prince and the gooseherd. And you are my lovely bride, Gülsün.'

Out of pure happiness, the royal couple were married all over again and the festivities lasted for forty days and forty nights.

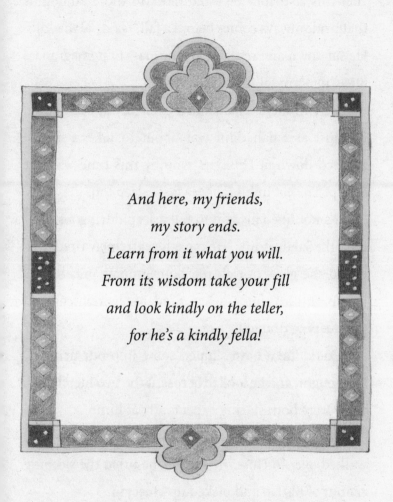

And here, my friends,
my story ends.
Learn from it what you will.
From its wisdom take your fill
and look kindly on the teller,
for he's a kindly fella!

"Let this last story be a reminder to those among us that pride always comes before a fall," said Salahaddin. He sat down and reached for the glass of pomegranate juice, for storytelling is thirsty work!

The two merchants smiled excitedly at each other. But just as Salahaddin was about to take a sip, he glanced down at Hüseyin, who by this time was fast asleep. The cat in his lap was fast asleep too.

"It's not like Hüseyin to fall asleep during a story," thought Salahaddin. "He must be extremely tired." He raised the glass of rich red pomegranate juice to his lips for a third time – when suddenly he remembered the sleeping draught.

"Could Talat have slipped some into our drinks?" he thought, and he looked across at the two merchants. They were both staring expectantly at him.

Salahaddin put the glass down on the table and walked over to Hüseyin. Gently, he lifted the sleeping cat out of his lap and picked up Hüseyin.

Talat came towards him with the glass in his hand. "Won't you drink some pomegranate juice before you go to bed? It would be such a shame to waste it," he said, thrusting the glass at Salahaddin.

"No, thank you," said Salahaddin, "I think I shall sleep well enough without it."

The two merchants paled and Talat lowered the glass.

"Now I bid you both good night," said Salahaddin. "I hope you will be comfortable in your room."

"Good night," said Rıfat.

"Yes, good night," said Talat, putting the glass down guiltily.

Salahaddin walked off towards the gallery with a heavy heart. "Hüseyin was right. These two merchants are not to be trusted," he thought sadly.

The next morning, Hüseyin and Salahaddin were woken at dawn by the call to prayer. "I slept really well last night," said Hüseyin. "In fact, I don't remember anything about last night. I don't remember getting into bed and I don't remember your story. You did tell a story, didn't you? I remember you standing up."

"Yes, I did tell a story, but you fell asleep."

"Really? I'm sorry. I must have been really tired," said Hüseyin.

"We were both tired," said Salahaddin. "Come on,

let's go and have breakfast. I'm starving."

Salahaddin didn't say anything about the pomegranate juice. He didn't want Hüseyin to worry about the merchants. He had promised to accompany them to Istanbul and he was determined to keep that promise. He would just have to be very careful on the journey. "Who knows what other tricks they have up their sleeves?" he thought.

Meanwhile, the two merchants were hatching yet another plot to steal the stone and this time they wanted it to work. The courtyard was a whirl of activity. Many of the other merchants had reached their journey's end here in Bursa. They had travelled the long dusty road over snow-capped mountains and grassy plains and sandy deserts to buy raw white silk. Now they would travel back with the white balls of silk to China, India and Persia, where it would be spun and woven into fine fabrics in deep blues, rich reds, blazing oranges, regal purples and rose pinks. Other merchants had returned to Bursa with beautiful rich fabrics and were taking them to the silk bazaar to be sold.

❖ CHAPTER 9 ❖

A groom handed Salahaddin's white stallion over to him. The two merchants were waiting for them outside. Salahaddin and Hüseyin nodded to them in greeting, and the three horses made their way past the colourful caravans until they saw the empty road ahead of them. Salahaddin dug his heels into his horse's flanks and broke into a canter and the two companions felt the wind in their hair once more.

They were coming to their journey's end and Salahaddin still didn't know why Hüseyin was travelling to Istanbul. He knew that the boy was upset about something because sometimes at night he had heard him crying.

He slowed his horse down to a trot, stopped by a stream and dismounted.

"Why are you stopping?" asked Hüseyin.

"I thought we'd wait for the other two to catch us up," said Salahaddin. "And there's something we need to talk about."

"What?" asked Hüseyin. "Is it about the stone?"

"No," said Salahaddin, "it's about you."

There was silence for a moment, and Hüseyin's eyes clouded over. He knew what Salahaddin wanted to talk about. He tried hard to blink back the tears but they kept on coming. He wiped a hand across his eyes and sat down on the grass with his back to Salahaddin, digging at the grass with a small stick. Salahaddin stood still and waited for him to speak.

"There was an accident," said Hüseyin in a small voice. "A fire. . . They told me to run and get help. We were in the garden. The baby was upstairs.

My mother went to get her. My father tried to stop her, but she ran inside. My father ran after her. Smoke was pouring from the windows. It was terrible. I ran to the village to get help but when I came back" – Salahaddin put his hand on the boy's shoulder – "when I came back, the house had burnt to the ground and my family were. . . Everyone said I could stay on in the village. I couldn't. I had to leave."

"But why are you going to Istanbul?"

"I have an uncle there. I've never met him, but my mother used to tell me lots of stories about him. He ran away to Istanbul when he was thirteen – just like me."

"And what does your uncle do in Istanbul?"

"He's a rich jeweller. He works in the fine jewellery bazaar. Maybe he works with the jeweller you are going to see," said Hüseyin. He wiped the tears from his eyes and turned to face Salahaddin.

Salahaddin smiled, and sat down next to him. "Yes, maybe he works for the great Osman Usta," said Salahaddin. "We'll soon find out. We'll be there in a few days' time."

"We will find my uncle, won't we?" asked Hüseyin.

"Of course," said Salahaddin. "Of course we will."

But deep down, he was not so sure. Maybe this uncle of Hüseyin's was not a rich jeweller. Maybe that was just a story Hüseyin's mother had told him one cold winter's night. Maybe that was what she wished had happened to her brother.

Meanwhile, the two merchants trotted along the road plotting and planning. "I know," said Rıfat. "Let's kidnap the boy and demand the stone in exchange for his life."

"And how are we going to do that? No, I have a more subtle plan," said Talat, with a greedy glint in his eye. Quickly he told Rıfat his plan.

"Very clever," said Rıfat, and he thought of the magnificent palace he would build with the money they would make when they sold Salahaddin's stone. These two men were dangerous, but the danger was not in their swords – it was in their minds.

Talat and Rıfat caught up with Salahaddin and Hüseyin, and the four journeyed around the Sea of Marmara until they came to the town of Üsküdar on the shores of the Bosphorus.

It was late afternoon when they arrived, so they looked for somewhere to stay. They wandered the narrow streets until eventually they found a caravanserai. Salahaddin left his stallion, which desperately needed new shoes, at the caravanserai with the blacksmith. Then he and Hüseyin went out to explore the town.

They walked to the shore and stood and looked across at the great walled city that had once been Constantinople, capital of the Byzantine Empire. From where they stood, they could see the Sultan's Palace and beyond that the dome of Hagia Sophia and the minarets of the Blue Mosque.

It was then that Salahaddin remembered the story his father had told him of how the young Fatih Sultan Mehmet had conquered Constantinople for the Turks several centuries earlier. And now he wanted to tell Hüseyin the story.

"Look over there," he said. "That's the Golden Horn. To protect Constantinople, the Byzantines laid a great chain across the mouth of the Golden Horn so that the Sultan's ships couldn't enter by sea. So, to the complete surprise of the Byzantine army, he took his ships overland."

"But that's impossible," said Hüseyin. "How did he do that?"

"He ordered his soldiers, helped by a number of cattle, to pull his seventy ships over wooden logs down into the Golden Horn," replied Salahaddin with a big grin. "Then his army conquered the city."

As Hüseyin watched the hundreds of small ferry boats and fishing boats bobbing up and down on the turquoise-blue sea that lay between him and the walled city, he imagined how Fatih Sultan Mehmet must have felt when he finally conquered Constantinople.

Salahaddin interrupted his thoughts. "Tomorrow we'll take a boat across to the fine jewellery bazaar and go and find Osman Usta. We'll show him the stone. Then I promise we'll try and find your uncle."

When Salahaddin and Hüseyin returned to the

caravanserai, the smell of roasting meat drew them to the fireside. As they sat and ate, Talat and Rıfat came over to join them.

Salahaddin stood up and drew the two merchants to one side. "I promised to see you safely to Istanbul, and I have done that. Now I would like us to go our separate ways. I wish you a pleasant stay in Istanbul but I don't wish to see either of you again."

"I'm sorry you feel that way," said Talat. "However, we will respect your wishes."

"Thank you," said Salahaddin.

"And thank you for keeping your promise," said Rıfat.

"Hey," said a man standing nearby. "Aren't you a storyteller? I saw you in Safranbolu at Cinci Han. You told a captivating story about a prince and a nightingale."

"Yes, that was me," said Salahaddin. The man slapped him on the back.

"Hey, everybody," he shouted. "This man's a storyteller."

No sooner had he said those magic words, than

a crowd began to gather around Salahaddin. Talat and Rıfat were jostled out of the way but Salahaddin could still feel their hard, cold eyes on him. He shivered. Then he saw Hüseyin pushing his way through the crowd. He smiled and beckoned him over. As soon as Hüseyin was sitting down beside him, Salahaddin cleared his throat and a hush fell over the courtyard. . .

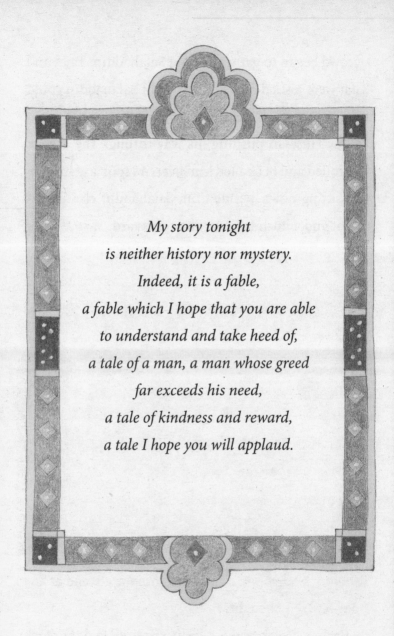

My story tonight
is neither history nor mystery.
Indeed, it is a fable,
a fable which I hope that you are able
to understand and take heed of,
a tale of a man, a man whose greed
far exceeds his need,
a tale of kindness and reward,
a tale I hope you will applaud.

The Golden Watermelons

Once there was and once there was not a farmer. One day in early spring, he took a walk around his farm. He was feeling happy because the long winter was over. It was a warm sunny day and the fields were full of flowers.

As he walked by the river, he saw a wounded stork lying on the ground and saw that one of its legs was broken.

Now, the farmer was a kind man who loved animals. He gently picked up the wounded stork and carried

it home. 'Somebody must have thrown a stone at the poor bird,' he thought.

Back at the farmhouse, he lit a fire and laid the stork

on a rug in front of the fire. He carefully bandaged its broken leg. Then he made a tasty soup for the stork to eat. The stork was clearly weak and needed rest.

Every day the farmer worked on his farm. And every day, he took care of the stork. Gradually the bird started to get better, and soon it was starting to flutter its wings again. But still, it was not strong enough to leave the farm, so the farmer continued to feed and care for it.

Then, one bright sunny morning, the stork turned to look at the kind farmer, before flying off into the sky.

Years passed.

One day, in early spring, the stork flew back to the farm. The farmer was in his fields sowing seeds for the next year's crop. The stork flew over the farmer's head, and dropped three watermelon seeds.

The farmer was surprised. He thought to himself, 'It must be the stork I took care of all those years ago.' The stork flew off and the farmer went on sowing.

Every day the farmer watered the seeds and watched them grow. The weather was good that year, so the harvest was good too.

In the autumn, the farmer harvested his crops. There were thirty huge watermelons growing in the fields. He carried them back to the house, one by one, and that evening he invited all his friends, neighbours and relatives for dinner, to celebrate the good harvest.

The farmer and his wife prepared a huge feast for their guests. And at the end of the meal, the farmer took a knife to cut open one of the watermelons. As soon as his blade touched the melon skin, the watermelon split into two halves. Inside, it was not red – it was golden. The melon was full of soft, pure gold! The farmer and all his family and friends stared in amazement. The farmer cut open another watermelon and saw that it, too, looked golden.

All thirty watermelons were filled with gold!

The farmer, who was a generous man, shared out the gold with his guests. One of his guests, a rich neighbour, was not a generous man: he was greedy and selfish.

'I wish I had as much gold as this generous fool,' he said to himself. 'I must find out where he gets these golden watermelons.'

The next evening, the greedy neighbour invited the farmer to his house for dinner, and the farmer told him the tale of the wounded stork.

'That sounds an easy way to get rich quick,' thought the neighbour.

The next day, he walked down to the river and looked for a wounded stork. He searched all day, but he couldn't find one. By the end of the day he was tired and angry.

Suddenly he saw a flock of storks flying low in the sky. They were flying down to the river to fish.

The man picked up a stone and he threw it at the storks. The stone hit one of the storks, and it fell to the ground. There it lay, wounded and in pain. Quickly, the man ran to pick it up, and carried it home in a sack.

Every day the man fed the stork a tasty soup and took care of it. After a few days the bird began to get better, and after a few weeks it could fly again. Then early one morning, it flew away into the sky.

Years passed, and the greedy man waited anxiously for the stork to return. Finally, one day in early spring the stork came back. It flew over his head and dropped three watermelon seeds. The greedy man was overjoyed and thought how he would soon be very, very rich. He waited impatiently for the watermelons to ripen.

Autumn came and the crops were ready to harvest. That year the harvest was not good. But the greedy man didn't care. The day the watermelons were ripe enough to eat, he picked them and took them back to his house. However, he didn't invite his friends to dinner. He was not going to give anybody else his gold. He was going to keep it all for himself!

He locked all the doors and drew all the curtains. Then he put the biggest watermelon out on the table and took out a knife to cut it open. As soon as his blade touched the melon skin, the watermelon split into two halves. But this time there was no gold inside. No – inside the watermelon was a swarm of angry bees! They flew out of the melon and chased the selfish man around the house.

They chased him round the kitchen, and they chased him up the stairs. They chased him round the bedroom, and they chased him down the stairs.

They chased him and they stung him. They stung him until he was as red and swollen as the inside of a watermelon.

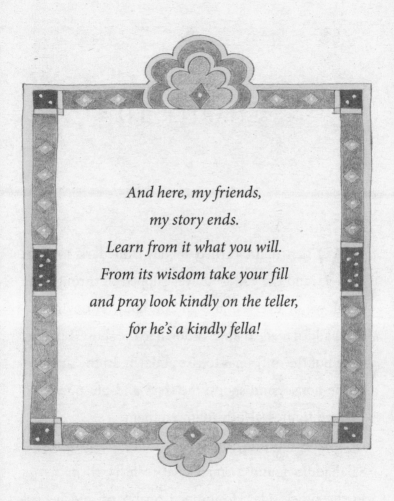

And here, my friends,
my story ends.
Learn from it what you will.
From its wisdom take your fill
and pray look kindly on the teller,
for he's a kindly fella!

❖ CHAPTER 10 ❖

When night turned to day and dark to light and the call to prayer slipped in through the windows of every house in the land, Hüseyin and Salahaddin made their way down to the shore. But they were not the only ones to rise at dawn. In the shadows of the houses and shops, the trees and mosques, two cloaked figures silently followed them.

As the morning mist rose from the Bosphorus, Salahaddin found a small boat to ferry them across to the other side. He jumped on board and helped Hüseyin into the small wooden vessel. Gently, the oarsman pushed off from the shore and began to row across the shimmering silver carpet of sea. Boats glided past them on either side; faces were masked and voices muffled by the morning mist.

Suddenly the boat slid into a thick patch of fog and Hüseyin felt a chill in his bones. A shadow fell over the boat, and he turned to see a boat next to them. In it sat two dark forms. He couldn't see their faces, but somehow he knew who it was. He shivered. He tugged at Salahaddin's cloak and whispered urgently, "It's them. They're following us. What are we going to do?"

The boat carrying the dark figures was now ahead of them. A feeling of unease spread through Salahaddin's veins. Hüseyin was right. "It's them," he thought. "They're still after the stone." But he didn't want to scare Hüseyin, so he said, "It might not be them, and even if it is, they are probably going to the fine jewellery bazaar. They have business there too, you know."

Soon the sound of the oars dipping in and out of the water was drowned by shouts of "Sesame bread! Fresh sesame bread!" and "Fish! Buy your blue fish here. Caught this morning, just for you." Their boat had reached the shore.

Salahaddin thanked the boatman and paid him, and helped Hüseyin out of the boat. Quickly he scanned the faces in the crowd, but he couldn't see the two merchants. "Maybe we were mistaken," he thought. Reassured that the danger had passed, he asked a bread-seller for directions to the fine jewellery bazaar. Then he and Hüseyin made their way through the sea of people to Mısır Çarşısı, the Egyptian Bazaar. The sights and sounds and smells of the busy port of Eminönü overwhelmed them and in the excitement Hüseyin forgot about the two men. He was happy to be finally in the wonderful city of Istanbul.

CHAPTER 11

Carried along by the crowd, they made their way into the wooden building that housed the Egyptian Bazaar. Huge, colourful sacks of burnt-orange saffron, pillar-box red pepper, electric blue henna and powerful-smelling herbs and spices lined the way. There were baskets piled high with dried apricots and figs, pistachio nuts and hazelnuts, pink damask roses and violet-blue hyacinths. Glass bottles and jars of jasmine and rose oil, orange and almond oil filled the shelves and their heavy scent hung in the air, wrapping the merchants and shoppers in a heady blanket of perfume. But best of all were the soft, square chunks of gooey rose and lemon, mint and nut Turkish delight dusted with snowy-white icing sugar, and the treacly toffee-brown whirls of walnut and grape syrup.

Hüseyin's mouth watered when he saw them. He stopped, and stared longingly at the tempting, sticky sweets. "This is heaven," he thought.

"Come on," said Salahaddin, laughing, and he took Hüseyin's hand and pulled him through the crowds. "We'll buy some Turkish delight on the way back – but first, we have some important business."

They left the Egyptian Bazaar and walked up a steep hill lined with little shops selling anything and everything, until they reached the huge iron-gated entrance to Kapalı Çarşı, the Grand Bazaar. Once inside, Salahaddin asked for directions to the fine jewellery section where all the jewellers worked. Hüseyin stood waiting for him and admiring the sumptuous treasures around him. Suddenly, his eyes rested on a man with greedy beady eyes and his heart missed a beat. The man walked towards him. Hüseyin couldn't move. He stood rooted to the spot looking into Talat's evil eyes. Now he sensed someone behind him. An arm slithered snake-like round his shoulder and he felt the sharp, cold edge of a knife across his neck. "Don't move," said a voice in his ear. "One false step, and I cut your throat." People were walking past them but nobody noticed the knife hidden beneath Rıfat's cloak.

"Ah, here's Salahaddin Usta," said Talat.

Salahaddin walked towards them, a worried look on his face. "Hello, Talat. Hello, Rıfat. I'm afraid we can't stop for a chat. We've got a lot to do today. Come here, Hüseyin. We have to go."

Talat walked over to Salahaddin. "I think you'll find that we're coming with you," he said. Then he whispered in Salahaddin's ear, "Rıfat has a knife with a nice sharp blade, and if you don't take us to your friend the jeweller, he will stab the boy."

"Why don't you just take the stone and go?" asked Salahaddin.

"Because we want to know what the inscription says and how much money the stone is worth. Let's go. And no tricks, or the boy dies."

Salahaddin looked across at Hüseyin. "Don't worry, Hüseyin. I'll get us out of this mess." Then he led them

through the crowded passages to Osman Usta's shop.

Before Salahaddin could say a word, Talat introduced himself to Osman Usta. "Good morning. We are honoured to meet you, Osman Usta. My name is Talat and I'm a respected jeweller from Egypt. This is my partner Rıfat. We have come to show you a stone which we believe to be valuable. Unfortunately, on the way here these two villains stole the stone."

"That's not true," said Salahaddin. "It's *my* stone. I found it in Trabzon and your old friend Ali Usta sent me here with it."

The old jeweller looked from one man to the other. He noticed the huge, expensive rings on Talat's fingers. "These two men are indeed wealthy jewellers," he decided. Then he looked at the travel-worn clothes of Hüseyin and Salahaddin. "I do indeed know a jeweller called Ali Usta in Trabzon," he thought, "but these two look like beggars. Who am I to believe?"

❖ CHAPTER 12 ❖

Just then, there was a cough from the back of the shop and a voice from behind the curtain called, "Father, may I talk to you for a minute?"

Everybody turned and stared at the curtain. "Will you excuse me for a moment," said Osman Usta, and he drew the curtain aside and walked into a room behind, where a beautiful girl with long ebony black hair and deep blue eyes was sitting. This girl was not only beautiful, she was also very clever.

"What do you think, Selma?" Osman Usta asked his daughter. "Who am I to believe?"

"Whilst you were talking, I took a peep at the three men. The first man is poor, but he has honest eyes.

The other two are wealthy and have no need to steal. But they have hard, cold eyes and I don't trust them. I think you should put them to a test. Then I will tell you who stole the stone."

"Very well," said Osman Usta. He trusted his daughter's wisdom.

"First, Father, call the tea boy and tell him to bring the police. Then, tell your visitors this tale and ask them in turn for their opinions. Then I will judge who is honest and who is not." And quickly, Selma told her father the tale.

The jeweller went back out into the shop.

"Sit down, gentlemen," he said. "Let's have some tea."

"First, I think we should have this villain arrested," said Talat, pointing at Salahaddin.

"I insist you all sit down," said Osman Usta. "First we will have tea and then we will decide about the stone." So the three men and Hüseyin sat down while Osman Usta went outside and spoke to the tea boy.

"Now, while we wait, I have a tale to tell you," said Osman Usta. And he began the story.

Once there was and once there was not a wealthy princess who lived in a palace with her mother and father.

One day, hearing that her grandmother was ill, the princess prepared a special soup to take to her. She didn't tell her parents about the visit because she wanted it to be a surprise.

The road to her grandmother's house wound through a dense dark forest of pine trees. The princess was scared. As she went, every woodland noise made her heart thump faster, but still she continued on her way.

All at once, when she was close to her grandmother's house, two thieves crept out of the trees and blocked her way.

'Give us your fine necklace, your precious rings and your gold bracelets,' they said, leering at her.

'Please,' she begged, 'my grandmother is ill and I must take this soup to her quickly. May I give you my jewellery on the way back?'

The thieves thought about their own grandmothers, and their hearts softened.

'Very well,' they said, and they let the princess go. She thanked them and continued on her journey.

"Now, Talat bey, what would you have done?" asked Osman Usta. "Would you have let her go?"

"No, of course not. The thieves were stupid. I would have taken the jewels immediately and then let her go."

"I agree," said Rıfat. "Those thieves were idiots. The princess would probably have gone home a different way afterwards and they wouldn't have got the jewels."

"What about you, Salahaddin? What would you have done?"

"I think they did the right thing," said Salahaddin. "It was good of them to let her go. Her grandmother needed her. They will be rewarded in heaven for that kindness."

Just then, the curtain drew back and the most

beautiful girl Salahaddin had ever seen walked into the room.

"Father, that man is telling the truth," she said, pointing to Salahaddin. "Those two men just want to steal the stone."

"Nonsense," said Talat. "This foolish girl doesn't know what she's talking about."

"Silence!" said Osman Usta. "My daughter is right. Your answers show your true characters."

Whilst they were talking, Rıfat had loosened his grip on Hüseyin and the boy had managed to free himself. He ran over to Salahaddin.

Seconds later, the police arrived and took the two wicked merchants away.

Then Osman Usta locked the door of the shop and they all went into the back room to examine the stunning rose-red stone. "My friend, Ali Usta was right," said Osman Usta. "The stone *did* belong to King Comnenus. The inscription on the back is in Latin. The stone is extremely valuable and now that I have read the inscription, I am pleased to say that the stone belongs to you, Salahaddin. It has chosen you as its guardian." He handed the stone to Salahaddin. "Keep it safe," he said.

Hüseyin and Salahaddin stayed on in Istanbul and Salahaddin became apprenticed to Osman Usta. He designed a beautiful gold setting for the stone and made it into a necklace. Of course Selma and Salahaddin fell in love, and on their wedding day Selma wore the gorgeous rose-red stone.

Everybody admired the magnificent ruby and the exquisite craftsmanship of the necklace. And after that happy day, people came from far and wide to Osman Usta's shop in the fine jewellery bazaar in Istanbul, and soon Salahaddin was famous throughout the lands along the Silk Road for his craftsmanship as a jeweller and his great gift as a storyteller.

They never did find Hüseyin's uncle, but Hüseyin lived happily with Selma and Salahaddin until, one day, he himself got married to a girl from his village whose family had settled in Istanbul.

Now, I expect you are wondering what the inscription on the stone said, so I'll tell you.

THIS STONE BELONGS

TO ONE WHO IS STRONG AND TRUE.

SO OF THIS TAKE HEED: STEAL IT FROM HIM –

AND BE PUNISHED FOR YOUR GREED.

The End

❖ MAP OF TURKEY ❖

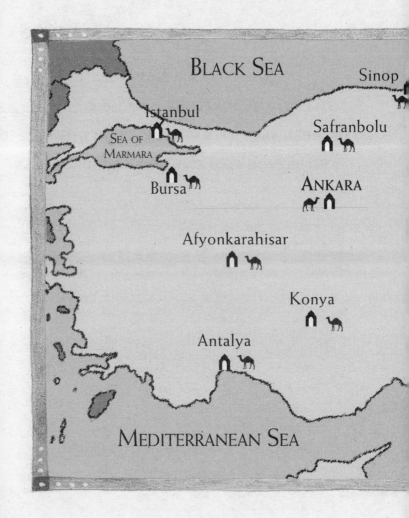

BLACK SEA

Sinop

Istanbul

Safranbolu

SEA OF
MARMARA

Bursa

ANKARA

Afyonkarahisar

Konya

Antalya

MEDITERRANEAN SEA

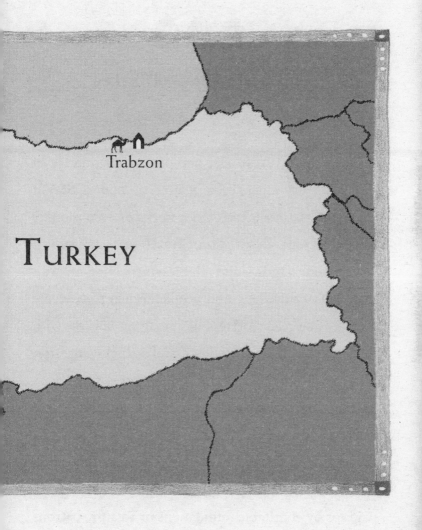

Trabzon

TURKEY

The Caravanserais of Turkey

Today, you and I can just hop on a plane and travel thousands of miles in a matter of hours, but in Salahaddin's time it took days, weeks or even months to reach your destination. Travel was dangerous. There were bandits and highwaymen lying in wait for wealthy travellers, and people needed somewhere safe to stay. So fortress-like lodging-houses with high stone walls, no windows, and a single huge iron door were built every thirty kilometres (one day's journey) along the trade routes. These fortresses were called caravanserais or *hans* (inns), and they could accommodate about two hundred people. You didn't have to pay to stay in a caravanserai. Everything was paid for by charitable foundations or wealthy patrons who wished to encourage trade.

Each caravanserai consisted of a large courtyard surrounded by one or two storeys of galleries and rooms and a big inside hall. All caravanserais had a *mescit* (prayer room) and most of the larger caravanserais had a *hamam* (bath house). We don't know exactly how the caravanserais were organised. Some people believe that animals were kept out in the courtyard while the travellers stayed up in the gallery rooms or in the covered hall. Others believe that it was a free-for-all, with travellers sleeping beside their animals wherever they could find a space. The covered hall was probably used during the bitterly cold Anatolian winter months for sheltering animals, travellers and their goods, while the open courtyard was used in summer. The travellers along the trade routes were mostly men and were of every nationality.

Each caravanserai had a wide range of staff: an innkeeper who greeted the new arrivals, allocated them places to sleep and told them about the various services available; housekeepers and cleaners; cooks; a doctor; an *imam* (religious official); a money-changer; a tailor; a cobbler; laundry workers; guards and police;

messengers; and a score of small boys who carried out errands and chores. There were also several staff to look after the animals as well as vets, grooms, saddlers, blacksmiths and stable hands.

Cooking was carried out in the courtyard and meals were eaten communally around a campfire. In some caravanserais, remains of clay ovens can still be seen in the raised platform sections.

After dinner there would be storytelling and performances by musicians, acrobats and bear-trainers. Merchants would exchange news and sell their wares. Chatter and laughter would continue long into the night. The new day would start with a morning call to prayer, after which travellers would either prepare to leave or stay on and rest for another day.

The earliest caravanserai is believed to have been built in 1210 by Sultan Giyaseddin Keyhüsrev I. There were over two hundred and fifty caravanserais in Turkey in Seljuk times (1077 to 1307) and thousands more were built in Ottoman times in the market areas of every town in Anatolia and, of course, around the Grand Bazaar in Istanbul.

So if you travel across Turkey by car or by bus, you will probably pass a caravanserai along your route. Some of them are in ruins but many have been restored for use as restaurants or hotels.

I hope you find the opportunity to visit one some day!

Sources

The traditional tales told by Salahaddin on his journey to Istanbul were chosen from stories sent to me by school children in Turkey and the Central Asian Republics of Uzbekistan and Turkmenistan.

The Salt
Adapted and retold from an Uzbek folk tale recorded by Dilshod Otamurodov.

The Prince, the Nightingale and the Silent Princess
Adapted and retold from 'The Prince, the Parrot and the Beautiful Mute', *The Art of the Turkish Tale*, Barbara K. Walker, collected from Neriman Hizir, 1961 (Texas Tech University Press, 1990, The Turkish Ministry of Culture, 1993).

All for a Wrinkled Little Pomegranate
Adapted and retold from 'All for a Wrinkled Little Pomegranate', *The Art of the Turkish Tale"*, Barbara K. Walker, collected from Suzan Koralturk, Trabzon, 1961 (Texas Tech University Press, 1990, The Turkish Ministry of Culture, 1993).

The Golden Watermelons
Adapted and retold from an Uzbek folk tale recorded by Adil Yoldashev.

ELSPETH TAVACI was born and brought up
in Bradford, and took a Drama degree at the
University of Wales. Moving to London, she worked
backstage at the Theatre Royal, Drury Lane and then
in advertising. After training as an English teacher,
she started work in Istanbul teaching English.
She now writes for Selt Publishing.
Elspeth and her Turkish husband live in
an apartment with a wonderful view overlooking
the Bosphorus and the ancient city of Istanbul.